With special thanks to Brandon Robshaw

For Dalton Chadwick

www.seaquestbooks.co.uk

ORCHARD BOOKS

First published in Great Britain in 2014 by Orchard Books
This edition published in 2018 by The Watts Publishing Group

5 7 9 10 8 6 4

Text © Beast Quest Limited, 2014
Cover and inside illustrations by Artful Doodlers
with special thanks to Bob and Justin © Orchard Books, 2014

Beast Quest is a registered trademark of Beast Quest Limited
Series created by Beast Quest Limited, London

A CIP catalogue record for this book is available from the British Library.

ISBN 978 1 40832 848 4

Printed in Great Britain by Clays Ltd, Elcograf S.p.A

The paper and board used in this book are made from wood from responsible sources

Orchard Books
An imprint of Hachette Children's Group
Part of The Watts Publishing Group Limited
Carmelite House, 50 Victoria Embankment, London EC4Y 0DZ

An Hachette UK Company
www.hachette.co.uk
www.hachettechildrens.co.uk

DRAKKOS
THE OCEAN KING

SEA QUEST

BY ADAM BLADE

ORCHARD

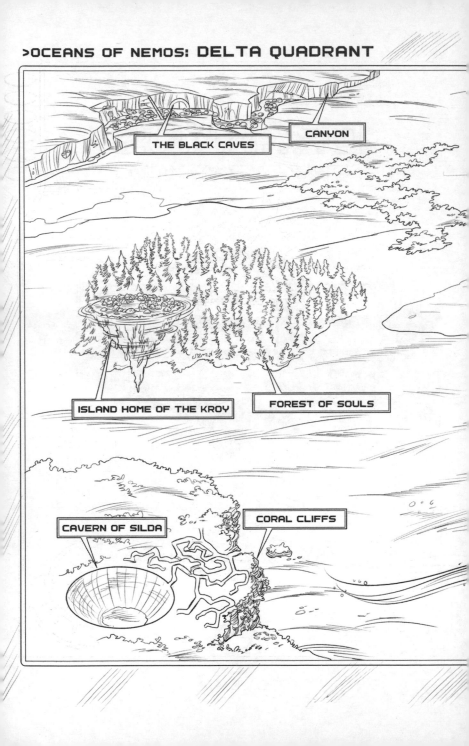

THE ADVENTURES OF THE LEGENDARY REGULIS

By Regulis

Welcome, reader, and prepare to marvel at the extraordinary tale of Regulis — Philosopher, Prophet and greatest of all the Merryn! Within these seaweed pages, I shall reveal how I was cruelly cast out of Sumara by the wicked King Salinus...and how I took my revenge!

In my wisdom I have joined forces with a fellow exile — the noble Professor, hated by his own people. We have devised a plan that will see our treacherous cities fall — first Aquora, then Sumara. We shall rule them both, thanks to the almighty power of Drakkos, the Ocean King!

Tremble, Merryn of Sumara. Your doom has come...

STORY 1:

ESCAPE FROM AQUORA

CHAPTER ONE

A DANGEROUS PRISONER

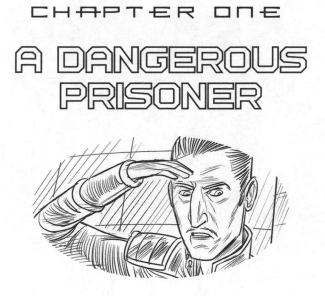

Max stood at the prow of his father's battleship with his robot dog, Rivet. His heart leaped as he saw the gleaming towers of Aquora in the distance. They rose from the ocean, glittering like silver needles.

"Look, Riv!"

The dogbot's eyes glowed red. "Woof!" he said. Max had programmed him to talk, but sometimes "woof" summed things up best.

Lia appeared at their side, shading her

eyes against the sun. She was wearing the Amphibio mask that enabled a Merryn girl like her to breathe in air. The underwater city of Sumara was her natural home, but she'd agreed to visit Max's city before heading back there. "Fancy a race to the shore?" she asked.

Max grinned. He loved a challenge. "Just let me get my aquabike! Come on, Rivet."

"See you in the water!" Lia jumped up on the rail and dived gracefully into the ocean far below with barely a splash.

Max ran below deck, with Rivet trotting after him. He passed his father, Callum, who was in his office tapping at a tablet.

"Max! I just need to finish this report before we dock – about how the fleet rescued you, Lia and your mother after you escaped from the Lost Lagoon. It seems more incredible by the second."

Max grinned. "Dad – can Lia and I go on ahead?"

His father smiled. "You can't keep still, can you? Always wanting to dash off on another adventure! Yes, go on."

"Woof!" said Rivet.

A short time later, Max was bouncing over the sea on his aquabike, spray stinging his face. Rivet motored just behind, propellers churning. Lia rode alongside on her pet swordfish. Spike was fast, and Max had to ride at full throttle to keep up.

As the towers of Aquora loomed larger, Lia and Spike began to edge ahead. Max twisted the throttle harder, trying to coax a little more speed from the bike. But the streamlined form of the swordfish eased further in front, and arrived at the docks of Aquora a few moments before Max.

Lia climbed up on the quayside, grinning, while Spike frisked around triumphantly in the water.

"All right, you win," Max said, as he moored the aquabike in one of the docking bays. He clambered after her, with Rivet clanking up the ladder behind him.

"I knew we would," Lia said with a wink.

Max took her to the main harbour, where

the big ships docked. The battleship was already anchored some way out, and Max's mum and dad were just arriving in a motorboat.

"We beat you!" Max said, as they climbed up the steel ladder to the quayside.

Max's mum smiled. "We weren't racing."

A shadow fell over them, and Max looked around to see an Aquoran Defence Officer. He was tall and thin, with a nose like the blade of an axe, and piercing blue eyes. His hair was dark and he had a thin black moustache. *Doesn't look too friendly*, Max thought.

The officer's eyes focused on Max's neck momentarily, then flicked to Lia and to Niobe, staring at their gills too. He wrinkled his nose as if in distaste. Then he nudged Max and Lia aside, and saluted Callum. "Chief Defence Officer North?"

Max's dad saluted in return. "And you are?"

"Lieutenant Jared," said the man. "I was

appointed by the Aquoran Council to look after the security of the city while you were away. On your – personal mission."

Something about the way he said it needled Max. "It wasn't personal," said Max. "We had to protect Aquora from Cora Blackheart!"

Callum put his hand on Max's shoulder. "It's all right, Max. We don't need an argument."

"No, because we haven't got time!"

Lieutenant Jared said. "We have a crisis on our hands. Our most dangerous prisoner, the one who calls himself the Professor – he's a member of your family, I believe?"

Max's mum nodded. "He's my brother," she said.

"Well, your brother has taken a hostage," Jared said. "A prison guard. And he's threatening to kill the man – unless he can speak to his nephew." His small, sharp blue eyes landed on Max again. "That's you, I assume?"

Max exchanged a worried glance with Lia. The Professor was the craftiest, sneakiest, most dangerous villain on Nemos.

What's he up to now? Max wondered. *No good, that's for sure.*

CHAPTER TWO

HOSTAGE SITUATION

The prison was a huge black building, with a single slender tower. Max remembered his dad telling him that the prison was one of the oldest structures on Aquora, and the tower was actually a chimney. But of course the whole place had been refurbished and equipped with the latest technology. It had just started to rain, and under the darkened sky the building looked cheerless and forbidding. *If you didn't know it was a prison,*

it wouldn't be hard to guess, Max thought.

Lieutenant Jared marched ahead briskly. "Come on, no time to lose," he said.

"How did the Professor manage to take a hostage?" Callum asked.

"He pretended to be ill," Jared said, "and when the guard came to take a look, he overpowered him and took his blaster."

"The guard shouldn't have gone in alone," Callum said. "We know the Professor is a dangerous—"

"I'm sure if you had been here, such a mistake would never have happened," Jared said sarcastically. "But you were off on the high seas having adventures, weren't you?"

"Now, look," Max's mum said angrily, "there's no need to be so rude. This isn't Callum's fault. You were in charge."

Jared stopped dead and stared at her. "You'd better be careful how you talk to me.

I am an Aquoran Defence Officer, whereas you are a crazy scientist who's been away for ten years – and turned yourself into a fish, by the look of your neck!"

"That's enough!" Callum said. His fists clenched and he took a step towards Jared, whose eyes went wide. Max knew that his dad wouldn't stand for hearing his family insulted – Lieutenant Jared was close to being knocked flat on his back.

"Dad!" he said. "We don't need an

argument, remember?"

Callum took a couple of deep breaths and unclenched his fists. "Let's just get this sorted out as quickly as possible," he said shortly.

"Very wise," Jared said. He went up to a panel by the side of the prison gate and placed his hand on it. There was a flash and a click, and the gates began to slide smoothly open. *Palm recognition*, Max realised.

"All right, let's go in," Lieutenant Jared said. "But not you!" He pointed a bony forefinger at Lia, who had started to follow him through the gate. "No Merryn allowed."

"What?" Lia said.

"This is a high-security environment," Jared said. "We can't have foreign fish-people skulking around it."

At that, Lia looked as if she was about to explode.

"Lieutenant Jared!" said Callum. His voice

was loud and cutting. "You are no longer in charge here. I am happy to vouch for this girl, who has done as much to defend our city as any Aquoran. She is coming with us!"

He took Lia's hand and swept past Jared, towards the entrance. Max felt a rush of pride in his dad. He, Niobe and Rivet followed, leaving Lieutenant Jared trailing at the rear.

They marched through the prison corridors, with Callum leading the way. The walls and ceilings shone with a bright, pearly light.

"Here's the prison control room," Max's dad said, stopping before a large titanium door. "We can talk to the Professor by video link." He touched the panel next to the door, which obediently swished open.

As they all followed Callum in, Max saw that the control room was full of state-of-the-art technology. There were banks of computers and video screens from floor to ceiling. An extra-large screen took up the whole of one wall.

"Be careful what you say to him," Lieutenant Jared told Max. "And don't make any decisions, understand? You have to leave this to the grown-ups."

Max didn't answer. He was afraid he'd lose his temper if he did.

"What an idiot!" Lia said softly, in Merryn, and rolled her eyes.

"Here we go!" Callum said. He sat in front of one of the computers, and the video wall hummed and lit up.

A life-size image of the Professor in his prison cell appeared on the wall. He stood behind a guard who was kneeling on the floor with his hands behind his back. The Professor's robotic hand was holding a silver blaster, pointed at the guard's head.

"Ah, there you are, Max!" the Professor said, giving a nasty smile. "Thank you for

coming so promptly."

"What do you want?" said Max. He didn't return his uncle's smile.

"That's what I like about you, Max – you don't beat about the bush! Well, I'll tell you. I want to get out of this prison. It's boring, and the food's terrible. So, if you'd kindly open every door in this place, I can walk free."

"I can't do that," Max said. "I don't have the authority. And why are you asking me, anyway?"

"Because we're family, Max! And families should help each other."

Max shook his head. "You're not family to me."

"You see this blaster, Max?" said the Professor. "At this range, it would splatter this guard's brains all over the cell."

The guard looked terrified. Sweat trickled down his forehead.

"That would be a horrible cleaning job for somebody," the Professor went on. "Why not save them a lot of trouble?"

Max's lips were dry. He had no idea what to do. He looked at his mother and father.

"Keep him talking," Niobe said softly.

She's right, Max thought. *At least I can try to buy a bit of time.*

"Why don't you put the blaster down?" he said. "Otherwise you might regret it."

Suddenly, the lights in the control room flickered.

"What on—?" Callum said.

Too late, Max saw that the Professor was tapping with one finger on the control pad of his robotic hand. *He's hacking into the prison system!* Max realised.

He ran to the main computer and searched frantically for a way to counteract the Professor's commands. *There – the Central*

Locking Programme! He was just about to click on Permit No Changes, when there was a sharp, echoing *CLUNK*.

"Thanks, Max!" the Professor said. "I knew I could count on you!"

He clubbed the guard on the back of the

neck, and the man slumped to the floor. Then he pressed his wrist-pad again…

And all the lights went out.

CHAPTER THREE

ESCAPE

The prison sirens burst out with an ear-splitting wail.

Through the din, Max heard cell doors being flung open, footsteps running down corridors and prisoners and guards shouting. "He's unlocked all the doors!" shouted Niobe.

"What – what's happening?" stuttered Jared.

Max's dad shouted at the top of his voice above the alarms: "Guards! Re-arrest every prisoner you can lay hands on!"

"We have to stop the Professor!" Max said.

"I know," came Lia's voice. "Let's go!"

"Come on, Riv – lights on!"

The dogbot's eyes shone twin beams of bright white light into the darkness. Max and Lia ran to the door with Rivet following.

"Stop!" shouted Jared. "I'm handling this!"

They ignored him and sprinted down the corridor. The dogbot's lights picked out prisoners ahead, like pale ghosts running through the darkness. None of them paid the slightest bit of attention to him. And none of them was the Professor.

"This way!" Max said, as they came to a crossroads. He remembered the way to the entrance from here. *And that's got to be where the Professor's headed*, he thought.

They ran on and came to the central reception hall. Here, prisoners and guards were fighting, locked in desperate hand-to-hand combat. Then Rivet's beams lit up a figure fleeing through the door at the far end. Max caught a glimpse of a robotic hand, glinting in the brief light.

"Come on!" he yelled. The three of them sprinted past the struggling guards and prisoners.

It was raining hard as they came out of the building. The Professor raced across the prison yard and through the open gates.

Max ran after him, as fast as he could pump his legs. Rivet ran alongside, but Lia couldn't keep up. Running didn't come naturally to her, as it did to Max. He saw that her face was twisted in pain and she was gasping for breath through the Amphibio mask.

"You and Rivet go on," she panted. "See if you can hold him up and – I'll – follow – as quick as I…can."

Max speeded up. Rivet's metal paws clicked

along beside him. They were gaining.

The Professor glanced back and redoubled his pace, reaching a flight of steep metal steps. He clattered down. At the foot of the stairs, Max saw the sea, a sheet of grey ruffled by wind and rain. *Of course,* he thought. *He's making for the docks.* He raced after the Professor, taking the steps three at a time.

At the bottom of the steps, the Professor turned and ran along the quayside, dodging past dockers and sailors.

Max and Rivet weren't far behind. "Stop him!" Max shouted.

But before anyone could react, the Professor ran along a floating jetty, frantically pressing buttons on his hand.

Where's he going? Max wondered.

And then something surfaced from the waves – a sleek, one-man sub. The Professor leaped off the jetty and clambered aboard.

He turned and grinned at Max and the dogbot. "I believe there's a phrase for occasions like this, isn't there? Oh yes, that's it – so long, suckers!"

The sub's plexiglass shield slammed shut, and the Professor zoomed away.

For a moment Max thought of diving in after him, but he knew he would have no chance of catching up. He ran back up the steps just as Lia arrived, so breathless she could barely speak.

"He...got...away?" she gasped.

"Maybe not!" Max said. "If we get my aquabike, we might be able to catch him!"

Two burly arms suddenly grabbed Max by the waist. Another man, in the uniform of a prison guard, seized Lia at the same time. Rivet started barking furiously.

"What in the name of all Nemos are you

doing?" Max demanded, struggling hard. "We have to go after the Professor!"

"You're not going anywhere," said the guard who held Lia. "You're under arrest, by order of Lieutenant Jared!"

"Why?" demanded Lia. "What have we done?"

"We can talk about that back at the prison," said the guard holding Max tightly. "Just come with us."

It was pointless to resist, Max realised. They would have to get this misunderstanding cleared up. "You wait there, Riv," he said to the dogbot.

"Yes, Max," Rivet said, and lay down on the dockside with his jaws resting on his metal paws.

"He'll have a long wait!" the other guard said, and both men laughed.

CHAPTER FOUR

A PERILOUS CLIMB

In the prison, it looked as if the controls systems were up and running again. All the lights were back on and guards were leading inmates back into cells, locking the doors behind them.

"Where are you taking us?" Lia demanded.

"You'll see," said one of the guards.

"My dad's not going to be too happy about this, you know!" Max said.

Both guards laughed. "No, I guess he won't

be feeling too happy right now!" said the one holding Max.

They arrived at a cell door. Lia's guard placed his palm against the entry pad, and the door swung open.

Max's parents were sitting on a bench inside. They jumped up at the sight of Max and Lia.

"Mum! Dad!" Max burst out. The guards pushed Max and Lia inside, and the cell door clicked shut behind them.

"The Professor!" Callum said. "Did he—?"

"Yes, he got away," Max said, lowering his head in shame. "He'll be somewhere out at sea by now. But what are you doing in here?"

"We've been arrested," Niobe said. "Just like you two."

"But why?"

"It's a stupid misunderstanding," Callum said, "which could be cleared up in two seconds if Jared would only listen to reason!"

The cell door opened again, and Jared stood there, flanked by two armed guards. This time he didn't salute Max's dad, but gave him an icy blue stare.

"Lieutenant," Callum said. Max could tell from his dad's tone that he was trying to be patient and reasonable, and finding it hard.

"You have to let us out of here. Or at least let us speak to the Aquoran Council. We've done nothing wrong. You'll need our help to recapture the Professor."

Lieutenant Jared gave a short, dry bark of laughter. "Considering that you were responsible for his escape in the first place, I don't think that's very likely."

"What?" Niobe said.

Jared held up his hand and started counting on his bony fingers. "Fact One, the Professor is a member of your family. Fact Two, the prison systems broke down after your son here – a boy the Professor specifically requested be brought into the control room – did something to the control panel."

"I was trying to stop him!" Max said.

"Fact Three," the Lieutenant continued, as if Max had not spoken, "the Professor actually thanked the boy for his help! Fact

Four, you have a Merryn among you." He glared at Lia, who glared back. "And two of you have gills on your necks – as does the Professor. You are obviously in league with the Merryn people, and you're cooking up some sort of plot to take over Aquora!"

"Don't be ridiculous!" Max's mother said.

"You can insult me all you like," Jared said, "but you can't disprove anything I've said."

"Oh, we can insult you, can we?" Lia said. "In that case…you've got the brains of a jellyfish!"

Jared turned pale and compressed his lips. "Let's put an end to this conversation. I'm going to discuss your case with the Aquoran City Council. You had better prepare your defence carefully."

He swivelled on his heel and left. The door swished closed behind him.

After the echoes had died away, there was

a silence, broken only by the drumming of the rain. Max looked up at the window hopefully, but he could tell by the sheen on it that it was made of vitrimant – a hi-tech alloy of glass and steel that let in light but was totally unbreakable.

Then he became aware of another sound.

Plink, plink, plink...

It was coming from close by. From inside the cell, he was sure.

Plink, plink, plink, plink...

"What is that?" Max said. "Sounds like water dripping."

"It seems to be coming from the wall," Niobe said.

Max moved closer to the sound. There was an iron panel screwed to the wall, painted the same sickly green as the rest of the cell. "It's behind that!" he said.

Callum suddenly clapped his hands. "Of

course! This building is hundreds of years old. They don't use the chimney any more, so they've sealed it off."

"But the shaft must be open," Max said, "because the rain's coming down it!"

"What's a chimney?" Lia asked.

"I'll show you!" said Max's dad. "Lucky the guards didn't think to search me." He took an electronic multi-tool from his belt, and applied it to the metal plate. A few moments

later, all four screws had tumbled out, and the panel fell to the floor with a clang.

Behind it was an old-fashioned fireplace, dark and dusty. Raindrops splashed into it. With growing excitement, Max stuck his head inside and twisted his neck to look upwards. Far, far above he saw a tiny square of daylight.

"There's our way out!" he said.

"Let me see," Callum said. He looked up the chimney. "It's pretty narrow. Your mother and I wouldn't fit."

"Lia and I could go it alone," Max said.

"It's too dangerous," his mother said. "Even if you get up there safely, you'll come out on top of the chimney. How are you going to get down?"

"Climb," Max said.

"I think we should do it!" Lia said. "The longer we're stuck in here, the more time the Professor has to get on with his horrible plans."

"You might be right," Callum said, reluctantly. After a moment's hesitation, he passed a card into Max's hand. "This is my Chief Engineer's Access Card – it could come in useful once you're on the outside."

"Come on," Max said to Lia. He climbed into the opening and stood up straight, heart pounding. There was only just enough room, but far above he could see the square of grey sky.

"Be careful!" said his mother.

Max nodded. "Follow me, Lia," he said.

The brickwork of the chimney was rough. Max felt for little holes and cracks then began to climb upwards.

He heard Lia below him, breathing hard through her Amphibio mask.

After climbing for what seemed like several minutes, Max looked up. The square of daylight seemed no nearer.

Keep going, he told himself. *Keep going.*

He tried to stop thinking about what would happen if he slipped. But he couldn't help it. *I'd take Lia with me. The fall would probably kill us...*

He forced himself to calm down. There was no way out, except up. Every little bit of progress brought this ordeal nearer to an end...

He took a deep breath and looked up again. Definite progress.

"Just a little way to go!" he called down in a whisper. It was lighter now, and easier to find handholds. Fresh air reached Max's nostrils. At last, his hands closed over the rim of the chimney, and he hauled himself out into daylight.

The edge of the chimney was wide enough to sit on. He leaned down and saw Lia's upturned face below him, streaked with rain and soot. "Grab my hand," said Max, reaching down.

Lia smiled grimly, and stretched out a hand to meet his. "Thank Thallos that's over. I thought we'd never..."

Suddenly she jerked as her foot shot out from beneath her.

She screamed as she fell.

CHAPTER FIVE

THE HYDRODISK

Faster than thought, Max lunged and caught her wrist.

The sudden weight almost yanked his arm out of its socket. For a moment, Lia dangled there, legs kicking. Max hung onto the chimney rim with his free hand – but he couldn't bear the weight for long.

Then Lia's foot managed to find purchase. The terrible strain on Max's arm eased. Now that she was taking half the weight, he was able to pull her to safety, his arm muscles

burning with the effort.

They sat on the chimney's edge, staring at each other.

Lia swept a strand of dusty, wet hair away from her eyes. "Well, that was fun," she said.

Max looked over the edge of the roof and saw the prison yard far below. "Now all we have to do is get down there," he said, with more confidence than he felt.

"That might come in handy," Lia said. She pointed at a rusty iron ladder that ran down the side of the chimney, all the way down to the ground. It must have been put there years ago, for maintenance work. Max let out a sigh of relief.

Soon, they were both safely on the ground. It was raining even harder now, and the prison yard was empty.

"I never thought I'd say this," Lia said, "but it's good to feel the ground beneath my feet!"

Max smiled. "We still have to get through the gates, though."

They moved towards them, keeping close to the wall. The gates were high and offered no handholds, and laser-wire fizzed and crackled across the top. Max had no idea how they would get through.

There was a rumble of a vehicle from the road outside, and Max tugged Lia into a crouch as a delivery van pulled up. The driver got out and touched the palm-imprint pad. The gates slid open.

"Now!" said Max, and he and Lia dashed past the startled driver.

Moments later, the prison sirens went off again. *Now we're on the run*, Max thought, sprinting towards the sea. He felt a small throb of satisfaction at how angry Lieutenant Jared would be.

Down at the docks, Rivet barked a welcome as Max ran towards him.

"Good boy, Riv! Ready for a Quest?"

"Yes, Max!"

Lia stood on the edge of the quay, holding her head, her eyes closed. She was using her Aqua Powers, Max guessed. And a few moments later, Spike's head broke through the water. He leaped for joy at the sight of his mistress.

"All we need now," Max said, "is some sort of

craft... Hey, I like the look of this!"

In one of the docking bays, held in place by two giant steel fingers, was a hydrodisk. It was a brand new model, state-of-the-art, made of gleaming red metal and shaped like a manta ray.

It's the fastest submersible of its size ever produced!

"Hey! You! Stop right there!" The shout came from a group of Aquoran city cops, running along the quay towards them. Jared must have already put the alert out.

"Let's go!" shouted Max.

He passed his dad's Access Card over the pad controlling the steel fingers, and they snapped apart. Then he jumped into the hydrodisk. As soon as Max inserted the card into the slot on the instrument panel, the engine purred into life.

"Come on, Riv!"

The dogbot jumped in after him, landing
in the passenger seat.

Lia leaped into the sea beside them and
climbed onto Spike's back.

Together they surged out into the ocean,

ignoring the shouts of the officers on the quayside.

Max felt a thrill run through his body. Another Quest was beginning!

CHAPTER SIX
PILGRIMS

W*ow!* thought Max. *This is even better than my aquabike!*

The hydrodisk responded to the lightest pressure on the controls, skimming through the water with the ease of a real manta ray. And it was *fast*. A slight touch on the accelerator sent it zooming through the water at incredible speed. The console contained all sort of hi-tech features. There was even an ejector seat button. Max hoped he'd never need it, but it was good to know it was there. He grinned as he saw there was also a detachable FetchPad – a small square tablet with a single button on it. He'd never seen one in real life before. If you pressed the button when you were away from the craft, it would automatically speed straight to you. Max nodded in approval.

"Hey, this is cool, isn't it, Riv?" he said to his dogbot.

"Cool, Max!" Rivet replied.

We'll have to be careful, though, Max thought. The hydrodisk ran on Celerium, a newly developed high-energy fuel that was extremely flammable. The tank was full, the fuel gauge said. If he hit anything, the whole vessel could go off like a bomb.

"Don't go so fast!" Lia complained. Her voice was picked up by the craft's external microphone. Looking in the rear-view scanner, Max saw that he'd left Lia and Spike far behind. He slowed down to let them catch up.

It was a little frustrating having to travel at less than top speed, but he didn't want to get separated from Lia. And they had a much better chance of recapturing the Professor if they worked as a team.

"Where do you think he's headed?" Lia asked.

"Well, let's see," Max said. He looked ahead through the glass screen, but there was no sign of the Professor – just endless green water, with dark seaweed waving in the currents and shoals of silver fish flashing past. On the instrument panel was a screen with the words LONG-RANGE SCANNER. Max touched it, and at once a 360-degree picture of the surrounding ocean appeared. In the top left corner, he spotted a small black shape that looked like it could be the Professor's one-man sub.

"I've picked him up on the scanner!" Max said. "Come on, admit it – technology's pretty useful sometimes."

"If it wasn't for technology, we wouldn't have a problem with the Professor in the first place!" Lia replied. "Anyway, which way is he going?"

"North-west," Max said. "That's the direction

of the Black Caves, where his old hideout was."

"But why would he be going there?" asked Lia.

Max shrugged. The Professor's base in the Black Caves had been destroyed after the battle with Kraya the Blood Shark – there would be nothing there except ruins.

The screen drew his attention again. A collection of dots had appeared, trailing after the hydrodisk. Had Jared scrambled submarines to chase them down already? They seemed too small for that, though.

"It looks like we've got company," Max said to Lia. "Let's go closer and find out who it is."

He swerved the hydrodisk towards the group of objects.

"Wait!" Lia said. "I think I know who they are."

"How?" asked Max.

"I can feel them with my Aqua Powers. I think they're Merryn!"

Max let out a sigh of relief. "I wonder what they're doing here."

Lia closed her eyes and frowned, focusing her powers. "I'm getting this feeling like... like they're on some kind of quest!"

"Just like us," Max said. *And maybe they can help us with ours...* "Let's go and speak to them."

He steered the hydrodisk towards the travellers, with Lia riding alongside. Soon he could see them in the pale green water: a crowd of Merryn riding on swordfish. From their long sharp spears and shields made out of seashells, Max guessed they were warriors. He slowed the hydrodisk right down, and the Merryn gathered around. They looked suspicious and slightly fierce. *I hope we're doing the right thing*, thought Max.

"I'm Lia, Princess of Sumara," Lia called out. "Where are you going?"

"I am Krillus," said one who appeared to be their leader. He was at the front of the group and wore a headdress made from white coral. "We are heading for the Black Caves."

Max saw, through the plexiglass dome of

the hydrodisk, that Lia looked as puzzled as he was. He spoke into the voice transmitter on the console. "But why? That's where hundreds of Merryn were enslaved and forced to work for the Professor."

"It is where Drakkos is to be found," replied the Merryn. "A living descendant of Thallos!"

"What?" said Lia. She looked amazed. Thallos was the Merryn god, the father of the ocean. A creature of ancient stories and legends. *And now he has a living descendant?* Max couldn't understand it.

"How do you know this?" he asked.

"The Prophet has proclaimed it," said Krillus.

Suddenly Max thought he understood. "Ah. This Prophet you mention wouldn't happen to be a Breather, would he? With a grey beard, and a robotic hand?"

Krillus looked blank. "Of course not. He is a Merryn, like us."

So it's not the Professor after all, Max thought. *Then who?*

"A Merryn who says he can introduce you to a living descendant of Thallos?" said Lia. "Doesn't sound very likely!"

"I can see that you do not believe," Krillus said. "Travel with us, and your eyes may be opened."

Lia came up close to the hydrodisk, and said quietly: "What do you think? Shall we go with them?"

Max thought about it. "They're obviously on a wild-goose chase, but they're heading our way. And they look as if they know how to fight – so if the Professor tries a sneak attack on us, they'd be pretty useful."

Lia turned back to Krillus. "We would be pleased to travel with you."

Krillus nodded unsmilingly.

The Merryn fanned out around the hydrodisk, and they all continued to head north-west. Max eased off on the speed to match their pace. *It makes a change to have a bodyguard*, he thought. *Normally on a Quest it's just me and Lia.*

The Merryn sang as they travelled – hymns in some ancient form of the Merryn language that Max didn't understand, but the harmonies were haunting and beautiful.

A ridge loomed up ahead. They rose over it, and a steep valley lay on the other side. The Merryn stopped singing. Down at the bottom lay the Black Caves. The entrance was a dark hole in the rock, partially blocked by bits of twisted metal, and chunks of rock and debris, like broken teeth. Max couldn't see any other entrances – they must all have been destroyed in the explosion when he was last at the Caves.

"Look, Max!" barked Rivet. Max followed his dogbot's gaze and saw an abandoned submarine. His heart leaped. It was the one the Professor had escaped in.

"Now what?" asked Lia. "Do we go in?"

"Oh yes," Krillus said. "We go in."

Max angled the hydrodisk down towards the entrance of the Black Caves.

All right, Uncle, he thought. *We're coming for you!*

CHAPTER SEVEN

INTO THE BLACK CAVES

Max landed the hydrodisk on the ocean floor with a slight bump, opened the plexiglass dome and swam out to join Lia and the host of mounted Merryn.

The area around the Black Caves was bleak and bare, a landscape of dark rocks and scorched sand. Max couldn't see a single living creature – no fish, no anemones, not even any seaweed. *As if this was a cursed place*, he thought.

"Spooky," Lia said with a shiver.

"It is not spooky," Krillus said. "It is a holy place." The other Merryn murmured agreement.

Lia rolled her eyes at Max, but thankfully the others didn't notice. "I'm going to leave Spike outside," she said. "Doesn't look like there's much room to ride."

"He can guard the hydrodisk," Max said. Spike waggled his head in agreement.

As the Merryn dismounted, Max swam back to the hydrodisk and got the FetchPad. "This'll bring the craft straight to me if I need it," he said to Lia. "Clever, don't you think?"

Lia shrugged. "Spike comes to me if I call him with my Aqua Powers," she said. "And I don't need to press any buttons."

Max shook his head. His friend was never impressed by technology.

Krillus and the Merryn were hovering

around the wreckage at the entrance, as if plucking up the courage to go in.

"Follow us!" Lia said.

"Come on, Riv!" Max said, and he and the dogbot accompanied Lia into the darkness. The Merryn pilgrims followed.

The water inside the Black Caves was cold and pitch-black. Max felt objects bump into him as he swam. "Lights on, Riv," he said.

The dogbot's twin beams cut yellow swathes through the black water. Max saw that there were all sorts of bits of wreckage piled on the floor of the caves – broken bits of computers and technical equipment. Objects kept looming up in front of him and he had to dodge them. It was deathly quiet.

"Do you think there's anyone here?" Lia whispered.

"Maybe," Max whispered back. The dark, silent atmosphere made him want to speak in low tones. "Rivet – switch on your Thermolocator."

The dogbot made a humming noise.

"What's he doing?" Lia asked.

"Activating his heat-seeking function – if there's any warmth ahead, any life forms, he'll pick them up."

Rivet's nose began to glow red.

"He's found something!" Max said. "There's something alive in here, besides us."

"Drakkos is near!" announced Krillus from just behind them. "We are about to enter his presence!" The rest of the Merryn gave an excited murmur.

Max and Lia exchanged a glance. "Do you think it's the Professor?" Lia asked.

"Might be," Max said. The thought of it made him shudder. "Which way, Riv?"

"This way, Max!" Rivet said. He turned down a side tunnel, and they all followed.

The dogbot's nose was glowing even brighter.

Max saw lights coming towards them. He tensed. Then he saw that they were approaching a shiny metal wall. The lights were just their reflection.

He and Lia swam forward to explore the wall, feeling for an opening. But it went from floor to ceiling and completely blocked the tunnel. *It's a dead end!* Max realised. He hammered on the wall in frustration.

"What is this?" demanded Krillus.

"Sorry," Lia said. "It looks like you won't be meeting any descendants of Thallos today."

As she uttered the word "Thallos", there was a rumbling noise. Max felt the wall tremble. Then it began to slide upwards, disappearing into the roof of the tunnel.

The tunnel was suddenly flooded with light. Max put his hands to his eyes – after the pitch blackness, the glare was dazzling.

He heard Lia draw in her breath, and the crowd of Merryn murmur in awe.

As Max's eyes got used to the light, he saw that behind the wall was a huge cave, filled with water and lit by pale, phosphorescent lamps. In the middle of the cave floated one of the strangest creatures Max had ever seen.

It looked like a huge, prehistoric sea creature, with a large round body, great flat fins, a long tail and an elongated neck like

a serpent's. Its head ended in a scaly beak, lined with sharp, curved teeth. The creature was undulating gently in the current, and its eyes were closed.

"Drakkos!" said Krillus. "All hail Drakkos!"

"Drakkos!" echoed the other Merryn. "All hail Drakkos!"

Max looked at Lia. Her eyes were wide in astonishment. "Could it be...?" he asked.

"I – I don't know," she said. "It...sort of

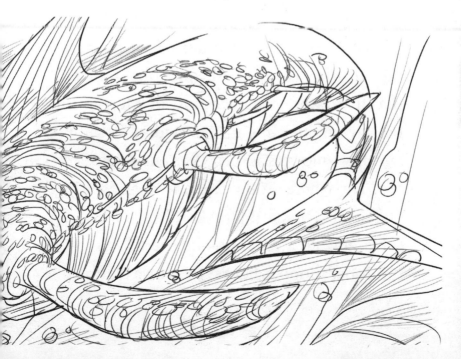

looks like Thallos."

She was right. Max had seen the statue of Thallos in Sumara. This beast *could* be related. *It certainly doesn't seem to be a Robobeast,* Max thought. *No harness, no robotic controls, no attachments...*

"Maybe this is nothing to do with the Professor," he said, bewildered. "But then, his sub was outside. What do you think?"

Lia shook her head. "I don't know what to think."

Krillus and the Merryn swam past, towards the creature. For the first time, Max noticed that there were already a host of Merryn in the cavern, kneeling in the shadows. Krillus and his followers joined them and kneeled too. The whole group began to chant softly: "Drakkos! Drakkos! Drakkos!"

Lia nudged Max. "Look up there!"

A robed, hooded figure stood on a platform

overlooking the cavern. *The Professor?* Max wondered. But no, something about the figure didn't seem quite right...

"It must be the Prophet!" Lia said.

At the sound of her voice, the figure turned towards them and threw back his hood. With a shock, Max recognised the face below. *Regulis!* It was him – the evil Merryn councillor who had tried to take over Sumara, using the Robobeast Skalda the Soul Stealer.

Regulis's eyes were wild and staring as he pointed at Max and Lia.

"Intruders!" he screamed. "Unbelievers! Spies! Arrest them in the name of Drakkos!"

The kneeling Merryn all suddenly rose up and swam towards Max and Lia. There was no time to escape. In an instant they were surrounded and seized by many hands, then dragged before Regulis.

"We must punish the unbelievers," Regulis

said, "in the name of Drakkos."

"In the name of Drakkos!" they echoed.

"Let us go!" Max shouted. "Look, this is Lia, princess of Sumara! If you're loyal Sumarans, listen to her."

"It's true," Lia said. "I am the daughter of King Salinus, and that man, who you call your Prophet, tried to become the ruler of Sumara—"

"We are not from Sumara," Krillus said,

"and we are not interested in your politics. We are a nomadic people, who travelled in search of Drakkos, and thanks to our Prophet we have found him!"

The other Merryn roared in approval.

Max struggled to break free from the hands that held him. But it was impossible. There were far too many. He and Lia were helpless.

Regulis smiled a horrible smile.

"Put them to sleep!" he ordered.

A Merryn woman came forward, holding a handful of seaweed. As she thrust it towards his face, a sickly-sweet smell invaded his nostrils. Max recognised it at once – it was the same sleeping potion Regulis had used on them before, back in Sumara. He frantically tried to twist free, to jerk his head away.

The woman clamped the seaweed over his face. The fumes overwhelmed Max. The cave began to spin…and everything went black.

CHAPTER EIGHT

FACE TO FACE WITH DRAKKOS

Max opened his eyes and was instantly dazzled by a bright light. He tried to raise his hand to cover his face, but it wouldn't move. *I'm strapped down*, he realised.

Squinting against the glare, Max saw that he was in a reclining seat, like a dentist's chair, with straps holding his wrists and ankles. In the seat next to him was Lia, in an Amphibio mask. Rivet was there too, chained to the wall.

Lia woke up and blinked. "Where are we?"

"I'm not sure," Max said. It was a large, air-conditioned room, with computers and screens all around the walls, giving out a soft electrical hum. There was scientific equipment everywhere, most of which Max couldn't even guess the purpose of: tubes and pipes, units with instrument panels and dials,

workbenches, a tank of green water which made a bubbling sound... "Looks like some sort of laboratory."

"The Professor must be behind this!" Lia said at once.

"I bet you're right," Max said. "Rivet? Activate your video function."

"Yes, Max!" There was a click and a soft hiss as the dogbot's recorder started up. If they could get a video of this place stored in Rivet's memory, it could teach them a lot about the Professor's plans. *If we ever get out of here and have the chance to study it*, Max thought.

The laboratory door opened. "My dear Max – what a pleasant surprise!" said a familiar voice. "So glad you were able to drop in."

The Professor stepped into the room. Regulis followed him in, unhooded now and wearing an Amphibio mask to breathe.

"What's going on?" Max demanded. "What

are you doing with that animal?"

"That animal, as you call it, is my best, most perfect Robobeast yet," said the Professor.

"It doesn't look like a Robobeast," said Lia.

"Oh, you noticed?" the Professor said. "Some people might say you're stupid, Lia, but I'd say you're just a little slow-witted." Regulis gave a dry chuckle beneath his Amphibio mask. "Yes," the Professor went on, "the beauty of Drakkos is that it looks one hundred per cent natural, but is in fact one hundred per cent robotic. Watch!"

Max's uncle turned and tapped at one of the computer keyboards, and a screen on the wall burst into life, showing a 3-D image of Drakkos. The Professor rotated the beast so they could see it from every angle.

Then he touched some more buttons, and the creature's scaly skin disappeared. Beneath it was a metal skeleton, linked to electrical wires which were attached to a large silver object in an inner compartment. *Must be a battery*, Max thought. *Amazing – it's the most lifelike robot I've ever seen.*

"Now, don't give your verdict yet," said the Professor. "Wait till you see what it can do!"

He stabbed at more buttons. First, Drakkos's tail began whirring round, so that the metal fins at the end of it became a blur. "Works like a circular saw," the Professor explained. "It'll cut through anything. So will the side fins – they're made of pure vernium. And look at the neck!"

The creature's neck straightened and extended to twice its normal length. It turned around on the screen so that it was facing Max and Lia. Suddenly a missile shot from its mouth, straight at them. The 3-D illusion was so strong that Max flinched and Lia cried out in alarm. The Professor and Regulis laughed.

"It fires torpedoes," the Professor said. "Go on, admit it – I really am a genius, aren't I?"

"You're a madman," Lia said.

The Professor gave a little start as if he had been stung, and frowned. "My plan's a pretty good one for a madman, I think you'll find!"

"What is the plan, then?" Max asked. He wanted to keep his uncle talking – Rivet was still recording everything.

"They don't need to know," Regulis said.

"Perhaps not – but I do love a *captive*

audience!" the Professor said. He turned towards Max and Lia again. "When my friend Regulis was exiled from Sumara, he very sensibly made contact with me. He knew I could help him get his revenge; and I knew he could help me conquer Aquora. There was a slight interruption to the plan when I was imprisoned – but that's all behind us now, thanks to you helping me escape, Max!"

"I didn't help you," Max said, annoyed.

"Of course you did. You maintained contact on the signal link just long enough for me to hack into the prison system! So now here we are. Drakkos is such a convincing Robobeast that all Regulis's followers think he's real. They believe that Regulis can communicate with Drakkos – and they'll do everything he says. It's very neat, you see. I supply the Robobeast, and Regulis supplies the army."

"Army?" Max said. "What for?"

As he spoke, he was secretly tugging against the straps that held him. If he could just work his hands free...

"Max," the Professor said. "You seem to be having trouble there – I'd hate you to hurt your wrists! Let me help." He took a blaster from his belt and pointed it at Max, then touched a button on the arm of the chair. The straps sprang open. He did the same for Lia, keeping the blaster trained on Max the whole time. "I'm sure you won't do anything foolish – you'd rather keep your head on your shoulders, wouldn't you? Now come along. I'm going to take you two on a little trip."

He motioned them with the blaster towards a door at the end of the lab. Max gritted his teeth and did as he was told – there didn't seem to be much choice. As they walked past, Rivet gave an electronic whine.

"Don't worry, I'll be back soon," Max said.

His uncle laughed. "Such an optimist, aren't you, Max?" He touched the door and it opened to reveal an elevator. "Going down!"

He gestured with the blaster for them to enter. Then he and Regulis got in too, and the door swished shut. Max felt his stomach drop as the elevator plunged downwards.

"What were you saying about an army?" Max asked.

"Oh, yes. Drakkos will lead an army of devout worshippers against Aquora in a surprise attack. Aquora falls. Armed with Aquoran technology, we then descend on Sumara and mop them up too! Regulis rules below the sea, and I rule above it. Neat, isn't it?" He looked at Lia and smiled. "Does that sound mad to you?"

"Yes," said Lia.

"It's crazy!" Max said. "You haven't got a chance of defeating Aquora, even with that

Robobeast to help." For a moment, he thought he caught a flicker of doubt on Regulis's face.

The Professor laughed. "You haven't seen Drakkos in action yet. Aquora won't know what's hit it."

"You are giving away too much," Regulis said. He sounded uncomfortable.

"Don't be silly," the Professor told him. "They won't have the chance to tell anyone."

"Why not?" demanded Lia.

"This is where you find out," Regulis said, as the elevator came to a stop.

The door opened. The Professor grabbed Max while Regulis grabbed Lia, and they were both pushed out into a circular chamber.

The elevator door closed, and the chamber began to fill with water.

"What's happening?" Lia said.

"Something bad," Max said. "Whatever it is, I don't think the Professor expects us to survive it. So we'll have to disappoint him."

The chamber was soon full of water. Lia tore off her Amphibio mask. Suddenly one whole wall slid up, and Max and Lia were sucked up a curving tube into the sea. But not the open sea. They were in a large, underwater glass dome. All around the dome were the Merryn disciples, floating in the water and goggling through the glass at them. The Professor and Regulis were there too, smiling.

With a lurch of his stomach, Max recognised the dome. It was the place where he had fought Kraya the Blood Shark. The hole in the side he'd escaped through last time was still there. The floor of the dome was littered with broken weapons – swords, spears, hyperblades, the remains of past battles.

"Follow me!" he said to Lia. Once outside they'd have to take their chances getting past the Merryn – but that was better than waiting in here. Every instinct in his body was yelling of danger. They began to swim towards the hole, but Regulis's voice boomed out.

"Behold, loyal followers of Drakkos! The two unbelievers will be sacrificed to the descendant of Thallos!"

Max heard a grating noise, and the floor of the dome slid away. From the blackness beneath, the enormous form of Drakkos suddenly shot up, blocking their path and creating a current that slammed Max and Lia against the side of the dome.

The Merryn screamed with excitement.

There was no chance of escape now. The beast's tail rotated and its razor-sharp fins twitched. It fixed its beady eyes upon them and extended its neck.

Drakkos's mouth opened, displaying rows of curved white teeth, like knives. It gave a long, evil-sounding hiss.

The Professor's most deadly Robobeast yet.

"Any ideas?" asked Lia.

For once, Max's mind was blank.

STORY 2:

ALL HAIL DRAKKOS

CHAPTER ONE

A DEADLY DUEL

Drakkos's neck shot out with frightening speed. Its head loomed right in Max's face, jaws snapping hard. The bite would surely have ripped Max's face off, but he had already tumble-turned and dived underneath the beast.

Drakkos turned and lunged at Lia. She kicked her legs and rose to the top of the dome – the Robobeast's clashing teeth just missed her feet.

Max swam to the floor of the dome, which

had slid back into place, and snatched up a broken hyperblade, just as the creature came swooping down at him again. He slashed at the monster's head, but it caught the blade in its teeth and crunched the solid vernium into fragments. A roar went up from the crowd.

Max's heart was hammering in his chest. How much longer could they continue dodging Drakkos? *We can't keep this up forever*, he thought.

"Help us!" Lia shouted to the watching Merryn. "That thing isn't a descendant of Thallos – it's a robot! That's why you can't talk to it with your Aqua Powers!"

The Robobeast swam around, keeping between them and the hole, eyeing them as if planning its next move.

"We cannot speak to Drakkos because we are not worthy," Krillus replied. "Only the Prophet can speak to the god's descendant."

"That's right," Regulis said with a smirk. "Only me."

The Robobeast lashed its tail at Lia, and she just managed to dive away. At the same time, its head arched round towards Max, and again he had to duck, escaping its teeth by a hair's breadth.

The Professor's face was twisted in a smirk of enjoyment, and his eyes were bright with cruelty. Just like when he'd shut down all the systems by remote control.

Suddenly, Max had an idea.

I've got a remote control device too!

He felt in his pocket for the FetchPad he had taken from the hydrodisk. Keeping an eye on Drakkos in case it made another attack, he pressed the button. *Let's just hope it arrives in time!*

Drakkos made its next move. Its tail rotated and it shot towards Lia – and even as she swam to the side its neck was already craning after her, like a water snake. She was pressed against the side of the glass dome, and there was nowhere for her to go. The Merryn spectators pressed their webbed fingers against the dome's surface, leering with bloodthirsty enjoyment.

Max had to do something. Dodging the beast's whirring tail, he swam up behind its head and clamped his hands over its eyes.

Taken by surprise, Drakkos bucked and reared, trying to dislodge him. Lia slipped to safety, while Max hung onto the Robobeast's head.

Drakkos shook wildly, hurling Max clear. He somersaulted in the water, and slammed into the dome. The sea seemed to spin, then as his vision cleared he saw the Robobeast swooping after him. Then Lia leaped onto the back of its neck. Distracted, it tried to turn round, struggling to get at her.

"Hang on, Lia!" Max shouted. "Help's on its way!"

"What help?" she yelled.

"That!" said Max, pointing.

The hydrodisk had somehow found its way through the tunnels and was streaking towards the dome. The Merryn crowd parted in panic as the craft zoomed through them. Max saw the look of rage on his uncle's face just before the hydrodisk broke through the hole in the side of the dome, smashing it wide open.

Drakkos writhed out of the way, and Lia was thrown downwards, thumping onto the seabed. The hydrodisk came to an abrupt halt just in front of Max, hovering in the water.

"Climb on, Lia!" he shouted.

He scrambled aboard – but saw that Lia was trapped by Drakkos. She lay on the seabed,

temporarily stunned. The monster loomed right above, its hungry mouth snaking towards her.

"No!" shouted Max. He hit the accelerator and flung the navigation wheel round so the hydrodisk hurtled in Lia's direction. As he roared past her, he leaned right out and grabbed her by the hand, dragging her into the cockpit just before Drakkos's teeth closed on empty water.

"Thanks!" panted Lia.

Max slammed the plexiglass roof shut. He aimed the hydrodisk at the jagged, enlarged hole and gave it full throttle.

Drakkos lunged at them as they passed and Max saw its teeth in terrifying close-up, grating against the transparent roof of the craft.

Then they were free, zooming through into the open sea. Merryn scattered out of their path.

"Now we just have to rescue Rivet!" Max said. "Then we're out of here."

"Max! Here, Max!"

With relief, Max saw the dogbot swimming towards them, metal legs churning up the water. A length of chain hung from his neck – he must have ripped it clean off the wall.

"Nice one, Riv!" Max said. "Now follow us! Stay in the slipstream!"

He turned the hydrodisk and headed for the entrance to the Black Caves.

Max heard the angry voice of Regulis shouting, "You cannot escape the wrath of Drakkos forever!"

But there was no way anyone was going to catch the hydrodisk. Max soon reached the entrance, where Spike was waiting for them. He flapped his fins in excitement.

"Follow us!" shouted Lia.

"We've got to warn Aquora about the attack!" said Max.

He steered the hydrodisk up above the lip of the canyon and hit full power.

CHAPTER TWO

DIRECT HIT

The hydrodisk sped through the ocean, heading south-east towards Aquora.

"I've been thinking," Max said. "Does the Professor really think he can take out Aquora? He knows how well defended it is. He's got an army of a few hundred Merryn – but that won't be much use against the entire Aquoran Defence Force. And we know Drakkos is no pushover, but how can it conquer a whole city?"

"You're right," Lia said. "But if the Merryn

and Drakkos attack, and they lose – what then? Who will Aquora blame?"

Max snapped his fingers. "Of course! They'll blame Sumara. It'll be war!"

"Which will weaken both cities," Lia said. "Make them vulnerable."

"And then the Professor steps in and takes over!" Max said. "He was lying to us about what his plan really was."

"We need to warn Sumara!" said Lia. "Maybe they can help – at least my dad can warn everyone about the fake Drakkos, so Regulis won't make any more converts."

She closed her eyes and frowned in concentration. A few moments later, Max saw Spike veer away and head off through the green water to the west.

"I've sent him back to my dad with the news," Lia said. "See? You don't always need machines to communicate!"

"Well, I do," said Max, grinning. "And speaking of machines, we'd better have Rivet on board now." The dogbot's paws were paddling more and more slowly. Max brought the hydrodisk to a halt, opened the cockpit and let Rivet climb in.

Rivet's iron tongue lolled out as he panted. "Thanks, Max. Rivet tired!"

The hydrodisk skimmed through the water. Rocks, coral forests and shoals of fish passed by in a blur.

Bleep-bleep-bleep-bleep-bleep!

"What's that noise?" Lia asked.

"We've picked something up on the sonar," Max said. He looked at the screen, which showed a group of pulsing yellow dots coming towards them. "Could that be Regulis and his Merryn, already? No, they'd be coming from behind..."

In the water ahead, Max saw a group of

Aquoran submarines shimmer into view –
black, streamlined shapes, like sharks.

An amplified voice came over the hydrodisk
intercom. "Give yourselves up at once!"

Max groaned as he recognised the harsh,
bossy tones of Lieutenant Jared.

"I repeat, give yourselves up. You are in
possession of a stolen vessel. Come quietly – or
deal with the consequences!"

Lia looked at Max. He shook his head. "We're
not surrendering. We have to get to Aquora so
we can warn everyone. Anyway, those subs will
never catch the hydrodisk!"

Max slewed the wheel round and hit full
power, zooming away from the Aquoran vessels.

"Open fire!" came Lieutenant Jared's voice.

He wouldn't really, would he?

But a moment later, a missile streaked through
the water. The hydrodisk gave a massive jolt.
Max and Lia were flung from their seats and

Rivet was thrown against the side.

"Ouch, Max!" said the robodog.

Max saw the underwater landscape twisting and turning in the windows as the hydrodisk went spiralling down towards the ocean floor. He clung desperately to the steering wheel, trying to right the craft, but it was out of control. They hit the seabed with a sickening thump, and Lia crashed into him.

There was a moment's silence.

"Are you all right?" Max said.

"I think so," Lia replied. There was a bruise on her cheek and her silver hair had tumbled over her face.

"Leave the craft immediately!" shouted Jared. "Or we will fire again!"

"We'd better do as he says," Max said.

He opened the cockpit and they swam out together. Max raised his arms above his head, but Lia stubbornly crossed hers over her chest. Rivet's metal tail trailed between his legs.

Four Aquoran guards in deepsuits were swimming down, with blasters trained on them.

"Come with us!" said the one in the lead. "You will be taken aboard Lieutenant Jared's submarine for questioning."

✳✳✳

"So," Jared said, when they were brought before him. He was sitting behind a desk in his cabin, leaning back with his hands behind his head, looking pleased with himself. Two armed officers stood behind Max, Lia and Rivet, guarding the door. "No doubt you think you're very smart, escaping from prison. But you're not smart enough to escape me."

"Lieutenant, this is an emergency!" Max said. "There's going to be an attack on Aquora – by some Merryn, but they've been tricked—"

"Ah, a Merryn attack! Just what I was expecting."

"Don't be stupid!" Lia said. "It's not what you think!"

Jared didn't even look at her. Instead, he said to Max, "So you want to make a full confession?"

"I'm not confessing," Max said. "Lia and I

are trying to stop the attack. It's the Professor who's behind it."

"And you're helping him," Jared interrupted again.

"No!" said Max loudly, fighting the urge to shout with frustration. If only there was some way to prove what he was saying. *Wait,* he thought. *There is!* He went across to Rivet and opened a compartment in the dogbot's neck. He removed the chip where the video was stored, and offered it to Jared. "Just watch this – it's a recording of the Professor talking about his plans – it's all on there!"

Jared eyed him coldly. "Very clever. A recording which you and the Professor cooked up between you, to put me off the scent? You must think I was born yesterday!"

He took the chip from Max, threw it to the floor, and ground it under the heel of his boot. With a cry, Max sprang forward, but one of the guards yanked him back by the shoulders. It was too late, anyway. The chip was in pieces.

"Guards!" Jared said. "Take these traitors to the brig and lock them up!"

THE COUNCIL CHAMBER

The brig was a tiny room with grey metal walls and no furniture. There was only just space for Max, Lia and Rivet to sit down on the floor. Time passed very slowly. Max sensed the sub moving, but without any viewing panels, it was impossible to tell which way they were heading, or how fast.

"What are we going to do?" Lia asked.

"Our only chance will be when we arrive in Aquora," said Max. "If we can somehow escape from Jared and his guards, we could get to the City Council building, speak to the Chief Councillor of Aquora, and explain what's going on."

After what seemed like hours, Max heard the engine note fall, and the submarine began to slow down.

"We're about to dock," he said.

Before Lia could respond, the door of the brig opened. Lieutenant Jared stood there, flanked by two tall guards.

"Come with me," he ordered.

"Where to?" Lia asked.

Again, Jared ignored her and spoke to Max instead. "You're going back to prison, of course. Where criminals belong."

"We told you, we're not criminals!" Lia protested. But Jared simply turned away, and the guards gestured with their blasters for Max and Lia to follow.

As they went down the gangplank and were marched along the quayside, Max was aware of passers-by staring at him and Lia – two children and a robot dog being escorted by armed guards. He felt a burning sense of unfairness. They were trying to save Aquora from being dragged into a war, and no one would listen! *If only we could make a break for it*, he thought. But there was little chance of that, with blasters trained on their backs. He'd no doubt Lieutenant Jared would authorise lethal force if Max so much as stepped out of line.

"Get ready," Lia muttered.

Max saw that her brow was furrowed in concentration, and her eyes were half-closed. *She's using her Aqua Powers*, he realised. *But what's she trying to do?*

Suddenly, there was a splashing, flapping noise. Max spun round to look at the sea. So did Jared and the guards.

A huge crowd of rainbow-coloured fish were leaping out of the water. They were like a fountain, leaping high in the air, twisting, turning, falling and jumping again, the sunlight flashing on their scales. Everyone watched open-mouthed, as if at some spectacular firework display.

Lia tugged Max's sleeve. "Come on!"

They took off, with Rivet scampering beside them. Max led the way, making for the maze of little streets behind the docks.

"Hey!" shouted Jared.

The boots of the guards came clumping up the street after them. Max's heart pounded. Lia couldn't run anywhere near as fast as an Aquoran and would soon be caught.

"Stop!" shouted one of the guards.

A blaster shot sizzled over their heads and hit a wall in front of them. The impact left behind a black, smoking patch.

"Here!" Max said. He grabbed Lia's hand and pulled her round a corner, then ducked into a narrow alley. Rivet followed. They crouched behind some dustbins, watching the guards gallop by at the end of the alley, with Lieutenant Jared bringing up the rear.

"Nice work, Lia," Max breathed.

"Lia clever!" Rivet said.

The Merryn princess grinned.

"Now – let's get to the City Council Chambers," Max said.

"Is it far?" Lia asked.

Max pointed to a giant, gleaming tower which dominated the skyline, head and shoulders above any of the other skyscrapers. "It's far up in the sky, if that's what you mean!"

Lia's eyes widened in alarm. "You know I don't like heights!"

***

They arrived at the tower out of breath and sweating. Two security guards in silver uniforms stood just inside the high glass doors. Behind them was a barrier of criss-crossing laser beams. Both guards had radio earpieces, and wore blasters at their belts.

"Yes?" said one of them. "What do you kids want?"

"Council business," Max said. "On behalf of Chief Defence Engineer Callum North. It's urgent." He flashed his dad's Access All Areas card. "See?"

The guard inspected the card, and raised an eyebrow. Max swallowed nervously. *It's only a matter of time before Jared puts out an alert to the whole city.* But the guard nodded and stood aside. He pressed a touchpad and the laser-beam barrier shimmered and disappeared.

Max, Lia and Rivet ran through the huge, glass-covered atrium. Just as they reached the elevator, Max saw one of the guards speaking into his earpiece.

Max touched his dad's card against the panel at the side of the elevator door. *Come on!* he thought. *Open up!*

Now both guards had swivelled to look at them. They unholstered their blasters and began to run across the atrium.

The elevator doors opened.

"Quick! In!" Max said. He, Lia and Rivet bundled into the elevator and Max hit the button for the top floor.

The doors swished shut in the faces of the guards, just as they reached it, and the next instant, the elevator was zooming upwards at a speed that made Lia clutch her stomach and grimace as if she was about to be sick.

"We made it!" Max said, as the elevator came to a sudden halt, and the doors opened onto the top floor.

"Urgh," Lia said, still holding her stomach. "Remind me not to travel that way again."

They stepped out into a long corridor, with a deep blue carpet so thick it silenced their footsteps. The walls were wood-panelled, with holograph pictures of famous Aquoran statespeople. At the far end was a tall pair of glossy double doors, with a gold plaque that read CITY COUNCIL CHAMBERS.

"Here goes," Max said. He knocked on the door and pushed it open.

The chamber was a massive circular room. It had glass walls all around, offering a stunning panoramic view of Aquora. But there was no time to admire the scenery. The councillors, who had obviously been in the middle of a discussion, went quiet and stared at the newcomers. The Chief Councillor stood up.

Max knew him by sight – he had often seen his picture on screens around the city – but he'd never dreamed he would ever be in the same room as him. Councillor Glenon. He was an elderly man with white hair and sparkling, intelligent eyes. "What are you

doing here?" he asked.

"There's an emergency situation!" Max said breathlessly. "Aquora is about to be attacked – by a group of Merryn, and by a sea monster, who they think is a descendant of their god, but he's not really—"

"Slow down," Glenon told Max in a tone that was firm, but kind. "Try to explain in a clear and logical manner."

"Look, the Professor's behind it all – you know, he escaped from prison – but that wasn't my fault," Max said. "And he's persuaded these Merryn to attack – they're not really our enemies, but they think they are..."

Glenon raised his eyebrows. "Is this your idea of 'clear'? They think they're our enemies, but they're not? And they think the sea monster is a god, but it isn't?"

"The descendant of a god!" Lia said. "Weren't you listening?"

"Ah, that makes all the difference," Glenon said gravely, and there was a murmur of laughter around the table. "I know who you are," Glenon said to Max. "You're Chief Engineer North's boy. We've heard all about your adventures. You seem to be a very brave and resourceful lad. But now I'm afraid you're letting your imagination run away with you! It's nonsense to suppose a group of Merryn would try to attack Aquora – with or without a sea monster. We are technologically superior. They wouldn't stand an atom of a chance."

"Yes, I know," said Max desperately, "but the Professor wants them to lose; that's part of his plan."

"Oh, and the Merryn want to lose too,

do they?" said Glenon. "And so does the sea monster, I suppose."

This time there was a louder rumble of laughter from the councillors.

"You've got to listen!" Max pleaded.

The door of the Council Chamber opened with a bang and there stood Lieutenant Jared with his two armed guards. He looked as if he was smouldering with anger.

"A thousand apologies," he said, saluting the councillors. "I can see your meeting has been interrupted by these two troublemakers and their stupid metal dog."

"He's not stupid!" Max said.

"Woof!" said Rivet.

"What is going on, exactly?" asked the Chief Councillor.

"I have come to arrest them and take them into custody," Jared said. "They're thieves. They stole a hydrodisk."

"Is this true?" said Glenon, gazing keenly at Max.

"Well, yes, but—"

"Then you may take them away, Lieutenant Jared," said Glenon, frowning.

Jared clicked his heels. "Let's go."

"If you'd just listen—" Max began, but the shriek of a siren abruptly cut across him.

"What's that?" Glenon said, over the

wailing sound. The other councillors rose to their feet.

A hologram flickered into life above the polished surface of the table. A miniature-sized Aquora hovered there, surrounded by a shimmering blue sea. In the sea, a crowd of bright yellow dots could be seen coming towards the city. One dot was much larger than the others.

"ALERT! HOSTILE LIFE FORMS APPROACHING!" said a robotic voice above the siren.

"Hmm," said Glenon. "It appears we're under attack."

THE BATTLE BEGINS

Max nudged Lia. "Follow me," he said under his breath, then turned and ran for the door.

Lieutenant Jared tried to grab him as he raced past, but Max ducked under his outstretched arm. He heard Lia and Rivet running behind him, then the furious voice of Jared.

"Stop! Come back!"

"Not likely," muttered Max. He reached

the lift and shoved the Access card at the touchpad. The lift doors opened just as Lia and Rivet caught up. They piled in as Max hit the "0" button.

Through the open doors, Max saw Jared flying along the thick blue carpet towards them. "If you don't come back I'll shoot!" Jared shouted, trying to unhook the blaster from his belt as he ran.

The elevator doors swished shut. A blaster shot hit the door with a bang.

Then they were plunging downwards.

The lift reached the ground floor and Max, Lia and Rivet ran out into the atrium. There were the two security guards, who immediately started to walk towards them, hands on blasters.

Max groaned. "How are we going to get past them?"

"Skittles, Max!" said Rivet.

The dogbot ran towards the guards, accelerating all the way. They stopped and looked at him in alarm, an instant before he crashed into them. The weight of his metal body sent them toppling over.

Max and Lia ran past the prone figures and out through the door. Rivet joined them on the pavement outside.

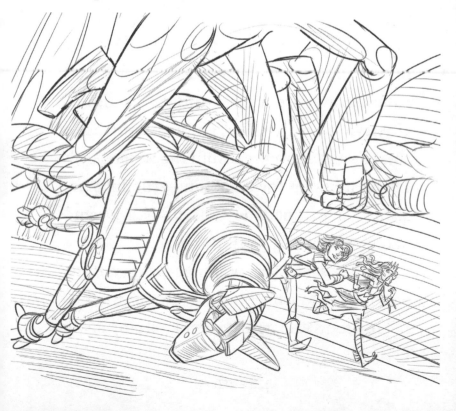

"When this is over, Riv," Max said, "I'll give you a can of high-grade engine oil, all for yourself!"

"Yum!" barked Rivet.

"Where now?" Lia said.

"To the docks," Max said. "We have to stop the Professor and Regulis – before they attack the city!"

Chaos reigned down at the dockside. Sirens blared and crowds of people streamed past, running away from the seafront and into the city, trying to get to safety. The titanium defence shield was being raised from the water slowly. In the harbour, the Aquoran battleships and subs were getting ready to sail, with Defence Force personnel hurrying aboard.

"Look!" said Max, pointing down into the water. Next to where Jared's sub was moored, the hydrodisk floated. It was like seeing an old friend again. "Come on!"

He and Lia dived into the sea and climbed into the hydrodisk. Rivet plunged in and scrambled on board after them.

A Defence Officer yelled at them from the quayside. "Hey! You can't do that!"

"Just watch me," muttered Max, as he slid into the pilot's seat. He pressed the start button and gunned the craft into life.

The next moment, they were streaking out to the open sea. The hydrodisk seemed to be working fine, despite the hit it had taken from Jared's sub.

When they were some way out, Max checked the underwater sonar and his heart jolted as he saw a crowd of shapes heading towards them.

"Merryn approaching," he said to Lia, and he made the hydrodisk dive deeper. "Let's go and say hello."

The hydrodisk descended into the dim green depths, water creeping over its plexiglass cockpit.

"There they are!" said Lia. Max saw a mass of Merryn coming towards them, riding on swordfish. In the lead was Regulis on the biggest swordfish of all, and the Professor on a black aquabike. At the rear Max made out the looming form of Drakkos, dark and shadowy, with the streamlined shape of a natural predator.

"If we can talk to them – somehow convince them that thing is a robot, not a real-life descendant of Thallos..." Lia said.

"Then they'll call off the attack," Max finished. "We can only try."

He headed straight for the Merryn army, speaking into the comms panel. "Listen, before it's too late! We're not here to fight, we have no weapons—"

The Professor turned and said something to the following Merryn.

They all raised blasters. *But Merryn never carry blasters!* Max thought. *They hate technology!* Then he had no time to think any more because sizzling energy beams were shooting towards the hydrodisk.

Max twisted the wheel violently and the hydrodisk banked away, narrowly avoiding the deadly rays.

"This isn't going to be easy," Lia said.

"You can say that again," said Max, as the Merryn took aim once more.

CHAPTER FIVE

THREE ARMIES

"Cease fire!" shouted Regulis, raising his arm high.

The Merryn lowered their blasters. Max felt a mixture of relief and surprise. "What's Regulis playing at?" he asked Lia.

"No idea," Lia said. "But it's probably not good."

"Drakkos – Ocean King!" shouted Regulis. "You were cheated of your sacrifice before. But now here they are again, offering themselves to you! Take them, Drakkos, for they are yours!"

The Merryn warriors steered their swordfish mounts to the sides, creating a gap for the mighty Robobeast to swim through. It moved rapidly towards the hydrodisk, its neck outstretched, its little dark eyes glittering with hunger.

Max turned the wheel to swerve away from it. But all of a sudden, the craft seemed to have become sluggish. It hardly responded to his touch on the accelerator. He glanced at the fuel gauge and saw that it was close to empty.

How can that be? It was full when we started,

and Celerium is highly efficient...

Lia must have seen his look of concern. "What's the matter?"

"The missile Jared fired at us – it must have hit the tank. We're leaking Celerium!"

"Is that bad?"

Before Max could answer, Drakkos opened its jaws. A sudden invisible wave of energy hit the hydrodisk. The craft was sent spinning wildly out of control, plunging down towards the ocean bed.

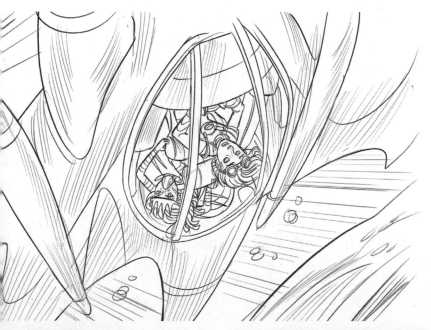

Max saw the rocky floor rushing up at him, and fought with the wheel, trying to pull out of the dive. But the hydrodisk had hardly any power left. It was barely responding. He heard his uncle's voice over the hydrodisk's intercom.

"Behold the awesome Aqua Powers of Drakkos, Max! Or what you and I would call 'pulse torpedoes'!"

That's clever, Max had to admit. *If Drakkos fired real torpedoes, it would be a dead giveaway that it's a machine. But the Professor's used technology to imitate Aqua Powers!*

Just as the ocean bed filled the glass screen of the cockpit, the hydrodisk finally, grudgingly responded to Max's wrenching of the wheel. They pulled out of the dive and started to rise again. But Drakkos was ready. It lashed out with its tail, and hit the hydrodisk with a sickening crunch.

Lia screamed as the whole craft was turned upside down. Max, Lia and Rivet hung from their seatbelts, as Max again fought with the wheel to get back on an even keel.

"Oh no!" shouted Lia. "Look!"

Through the cockpit windscreen, Max saw a thick cloud of yellow liquid blossoming out behind them.

"It's hit the fuel canisters!" Max said. *We're losing Celerium even faster. And when it's all gone, we'll be helpless!*

Just then, a silver shape flashed in front of the plexiglass, then doubled back and looked in at them.

"Spike!" yelled Lia.

Behind the swordfish, Max saw more Merryn arriving, also mounted on swordfish. They were led by the tall figure of King Salinus, Lia's father. There were more of them than Regulis's followers. They came to a halt, hovering between the hydrodisk and Drakkos. The Robobeast hung in the water, swishing its tail, as if uncertain how to deal with the newcomers.

"Phew!" Max said. "I reckon we've just been saved."

"I knew my father would get here in time somehow!" Lia said.

King Salinus rode up beside the hydrodisk and raised his coral sword in greeting to Lia and Max. Lia waved back, smiling. Then Salinus turned to face Regulis.

"Disband your warriors at once," he commanded. "Attacking Aquora will only cause trouble. It was a mistake to let you go, Regulis – I should have left you to rot in jail!"

"Well, you didn't," Regulis said, "and Drakkos be thanked for it. I'm not disbanding my army, so you'd better get out of our way."

"If you don't lay down your arms now, we will be forced to overpower you!"

"Overpower us?" said Regulis. "We've got Drakkos on our side – the living descendant of Thallos! We're invincible!"

"I gave you fair warning," King Salinus said. "Merryn of Sumara – attack!"

But the Sumaran warriors hesitated, gazing at the huge figure of Drakkos – and Max saw expressions of awe on their faces.

"Could it really be...?" he heard one of them say.

Lia shouted into the intercom panel. "It's not a real creature! It's just a robot, made to look like an animal. Tell them, Dad!"

"Well..." Salinus looked at Drakkos doubtfully. "It does look real. If it *is* a descendant of Thallos..."

"It's not!" shouted Lia again.

"Look out," Max said. "We've got company."

Out of the corner of his eye, Max saw a movement on the sonar screen. Several large dots were approaching fast. He turned and looked through the plexiglass. The Aquoran submarine fleet was bearing down on them. Lieutenant Jared's large, sleek sub was at the front, with a line of other underwater craft fanning out behind it.

"This is an order to all Merryn!" Jared's

voice boomed out. "Surrender immediately, and you will be treated as prisoners of war. Give up the monster to us so that it can be destroyed. You have one minute to comply!"

"Never!" said Regulis. Several of his warriors shook their spears at the Aquoran fleet.

"Lieutenant Jared," Max said into the intercom panel. "Please, there's no need to fight the Merryn. They've been tricked. It's my uncle you should arrest."

"I fully intend to arrest him," Jared said.

The Professor laughed. "Good luck with that!"

"As I shall arrest all his Merryn friends, and you too, Max," Jared said. "You can all be in prison together! Thirty seconds."

"We did not come to fight you!" King Salinus shouted. "But if it is a battle between Merryn and Aquorans, I will fight for my

people. You will have to defeat all of us!"

"Don't worry, we will," Jared said. "Twenty seconds."

"Woof!" said Rivet, tail between his legs.

"What do we do?" asked Lia. "If only we could somehow prove to them that Drakkos is a Robobeast!"

Her words sparked an idea in Max's mind.

"Ten seconds," Jared said.

"I think I've got a plan," Max said.

CHAPTER SIX

FURY OF DRAKKOS

"Five!" said Jared.

Max brought the hydrodisk round to face Drakkos. The Robobeast gnashed its teeth and extended its neck towards them.

There was hardly any fuel left, but there might be just enough for one manoeuvre. Max stamped on the accelerator and drove straight at Drakkos.

Lieutenant Jared stopped counting. "What are you doing?" he shouted.

Max saw Drakkos looming. Its dark eyes stared straight at him and its razor-toothed jaws were open. At the last moment, Max wrenched the navigation wheel upwards and soared above the Robobeast. Then he punched a button to release the remaining fuel load.

A cloud of yellow Celerium spilled over the Robobeast.

"Interesting," Lia said. "Now what?"

"This," said Max. He slammed the navigation wheel anti-clockwise, so that the craft spun and pointed at Drakkos again. The Robobeast was barely visible through the drifting cloud of fuel. Max hit the trigger for the torpedoes.

Two missiles streaked through the water and smacked into Drakkos.

THUD-THUD!

WHOOOMPH!

The Celerium cloud exploded in a massive,
dazzling flash.

The force of the detonation swept the
hydrodisk up and tossed it around. All Max
could see, as he was hurled sideways, was a
wall of bright green fire.

Then, through the flames, he saw Drakkos's
great rounded head lunging towards them.

"We have to bail!" Max shouted. He hit the ejector button. The plexiglass dome flew open and he, Lia and Rivet were flung out into the water.

Frantically swimming clear, Max looked down and saw Drakkos take the hydrodisk in its jaws and crunch it up like a biscuit. Green flames flickered around the monster's head.

"Look!" Lia said. "It's peeling!"

She was right. Melted by the heat, the

Robobeast's synthetic skin was shrivelling away. Max could see the steel skeleton underneath, the bladed metal fins, the tube of the energy cannon in its throat.

A confused roar rose up from the Merryn followers. They looked more and more horrified as Drakkos's robotics were revealed.

"We told you it was a robot!" Lia yelled. But Max didn't think they heard her. They were too busy shouting at Regulis.

"It never was a descendant of Thallos!"

"False prophet!"

"You lied to us!"

"No, I didn't," Regulis protested. He pointed an accusing finger at the Professor. "It was him! He deceived me!"

The Merryn all turned to stare at Max's uncle.

There was a moment's pause, as if no one quite knew what to do next.

Then the Professor twisted the throttle of his aquabike. "Drakkos!" he shouted. "Attack!" Then he zoomed away.

The Robobeast was no longer aflame. Its flesh had all been burned away and it was clearly a huge, metal, fire-blackened robot. Its tail became an invisible blur as it rotated, and Drakkos plunged straight into the crowd of Merryn.

They scattered wildly, as the monster's fins slashed at them and their swordfish.

King Salinus and some of his warriors fought back, hacking at the Robobeast with their coral swords. But their swords bounced off its metal frame, and a pulse from its energy cannon sent them flying.

"We have to do something!" Max said.

"I'm doing it!" Lia said. She leaped onto Spike's back. Max jumped on behind her and they swam closer to the Robobeast, which had gone totally berserk. *It's going after the Merryn like a cat after mice*, Max thought. As they approached, it caught one of the fleeing Merryn in its metal jaws.

"There has to be a way to switch it off!" Lia said.

Max spotted what looked like a control unit at the back of the Robobeast's neck.

"Bring us in closer!" he said.

Using her Aqua Powers, Lia guided Spike to a point just behind the Robobeast's head.

"I'm going down!" Max said. He slipped off Spike's back and landed on his hands and knees on top of Drakkos. The Robobeast's ridged metal neck felt hard and spiky. It didn't seem to notice him – it was still busy chewing the unfortunate Merryn it had caught.

Max inched forward. There was the control unit just in front of him: a black box. He was just reaching for it when he felt a slight jolt, and a pair of webbed feet landed right in front of him.

He looked up. It was Regulis. He was holding a long, curved sword fashioned from blood-red coral. And he was smiling.

"I still have a score to settle with you, Breather boy!" he said.

"I don't have a sword!" said Max.

"Oh, good – this will be easy, then!" Regulis said – and slashed at Max with his blade.

Max ducked, feeling the blade swish over his head. He backed away. *I can't fight without a sword. But how am I going to stop Drakkos?*

Regulis came towards him, forcing Max back over the steel struts of Drakkos's back. Further and further away from the control unit.

Suddenly, there was a blur of motion beside him. King Salinus darted by on his swordfish, holding his gleaming white coral sword hilt-first towards Max. "Take this!"

"Thanks!" Max said – and grabbed the sword just in time to parry a lunge from Regulis.

Max swiped back. But Regulis easily beat

the attack away. *He's been practising since we last fought*, Max thought.

"Come on, Max!" shouted Lia.

Again, Max had to parry a sudden lunge, which was aimed straight for his heart. How much longer could he keep this up?

As he desperately defended himself, part of his brain noticed that they were drifting closer to the Aquoran fleet. Most of the Merryn were a safe distance away now, and perhaps Drakkos was looking for something else to attack. Max saw that Lieutenant Jared's submarine was the nearest.

Drakkos opened its mouth and sent an energy pulse towards it. The shock rocked the body beneath Max's feet, and he struggled for balance. Jared's sub almost turned over as the blow struck.

"Aaargh!" Jared's voice came over the intercom. He sounded scared. "We're under attack! Open fire on the robot! Fire at will!"

"But we'll hit the boy, sir!"

"Just do it!" came Jared's panicked voice. Then his submarine swerved in the water, fleeing in a stream of bubbles.

Max felt a sudden jolt as Regulis's sword collided with his, twisting Max's weapon out of his hand. He cursed himself for being distracted.

"I think I have you where I want you," Regulis said softly.

Max backed away. His heel caught between the steel ridges of Drakkos's skeleton, and he fell on his back.

Regulis stood over him, aiming his sword at Max's throat.

"Any last words?" said the Merryn.

CHAPTER SEVEN

HONOUR AND DISHONOUR

A big metal object came flying out of nowhere and smashed into Regulis's side.

Regulis let out a yelp of surprise and turned a no-hands cartwheel. His sword slipped from his hand and went drifting down towards the seabed.

"Max!" barked Rivet. "Save Max!"

"Yes, you did," Max said, getting to his feet. "Good boy! If we get out of this alive, you're getting *two* cans of engine oil!"

"You have to get away from there!" Lia called, coming in close on Spike. "Before the Aquoran fleet opens fire! Here, jump on."

"Wait!" Max said. "I still need to deprogramme Drakkos. In case the missiles don't stop it."

"But there's no time!" said Lia.

The Aquoran subs had all lined to face Drakkos. Max crouched in front of the control unit. As if sensing what was about to happen, Drakkos started to buck and writhe, the steel rods of its neck rippling. Max held on tight with one hand. With the other he felt the black box. If he could get inside he could power down the battery. But the box was perfectly smooth and solid. And he had nothing to smash it with...

Wait, he thought. *Batteries. Electro-magnetic. If I touch it with something magnetic, that should reverse the field and power it down!*

He thrust his hand into his pocket and pulled out his dad's Access card, with the magnetised strip. He pressed it against the black box.

For a moment, Drakkos continued to buck.

Then its movements right slowed down. It made a noise like a sort of electronic sigh.

It stopped moving.

Then Max saw that the missile-launch tubes of the Aquoran subs had all opened, like hungry mouths.

"Get out of there, Max!" shouted Lia.

Max kicked off and grabbed Spike's tailfin. Spike shot away – just before a whole salvo of missiles smacked into Drakkos.

SMASHCRASHBASHWWOOGGHHH!

There was a massive orange and red explosion. Even as Spike swam away at top speed, Max felt the heat of it chasing them, vaporising the water into bubbles of steam.

He looked back. As the flames and the turbulence cleared, Max saw the motionless form of Drakkos drifting down to the ocean floor. It was still in one piece, hardly damaged by the explosion but no longer functioning.

"Wow!" Max said. "I'm glad that's over!"

A sudden thought struck him. *Maybe it isn't over?*

"Where's the Professor?" he said.

"It's all right," Lia said. "We've got him."

Max followed the direction of Lia's finger and saw that the Professor had been captured by King Salinus and two of his warriors. The warriors held him by the shoulders and Salinus was pointing his sword at the back of the Professor's neck, as they rode their swordfish towards the Aquoran fleet.

"And Regulis?" Max said.

"He got away, I think," Lia said.

"Well, I guess he won't be much of a threat without the Professor, will he?" Max said.

"I hope not," said Lia.

Max kicked towards Rivet. "Let's get back to Aquora. I think we deserve a rest!"

Max walked into the City Council Chambers with his mum and dad and Lia and Rivet. He was wearing his best clothes, which weren't very comfortable, but his mother had insisted. Every head in the room turned to look at them as they entered, and Max felt both proud and shy.

It was the day after the battle. A grand reception was being held in the Chambers, to celebrate the Aquoran and Merryn victory over the Professor's evil scheme. The Professor was safely locked up again, and Max's parents, of course, had been freed the moment the Aquoran fleet returned. Councillor Glenon had apologised to them, and to Max for not believing his story.

Waiters went round with drinks and trays of tempting titbits – including seaweed cakes for the Merryn visitors. Lia's father and his closest advisers were the guests of honour. They all wore Amphibio masks, and exclaimed with delight at the wonderful view through the windows of the sparkling city of Aquora, and the boundless blue sea that surrounded it.

"Max!" barked Rivet. "Engine oil!"

Max laughed. "Don't worry, Riv, I haven't forgotten! After the reception."

Councillor Glenon tapped the side of his glass. Silence fell.

"I have a few words to say – but don't worry, I'll be brief. We owe a debt of thanks to our Merryn friends. In the past there has been misunderstanding between our peoples. But recent events have shown we can work together – not only was war averted, but we must thank King Salinus for capturing the enemy of our city, the Professor! It gives me great pleasure to award the Merryn king the highest honour that Aquora can bestow, the

Gold Medal for Gallantry."

He beckoned to King Salinus, who came forward and bowed his head. Glenon slipped the shining medal on its scarlet ribbon over his head, to the applause of the whole room. Max clapped till his hands were sore. He was aware of Lia beaming with pride beside him.

King Salinus turned to face the room. "Thank you for this honour. I hope our peoples can learn more from each other, and

would like to suggest that we each send an ambassador to the other's city."

There was more applause. Glenon nodded agreement.

"But I should say," Salinus went on, "that I am not truly deserving of this medal. It was really Max, and my daughter Lia, who saved your city."

"Hear hear!" said Max's mum and dad loudly, much to his embarrassment.

"Three cheers for Max and Lia!" Councillor Glenon said. "Hip hip..."

"Hooray!" the whole room shouted. Max felt himself blushing.

"But let me end by turning to another, less happy matter," said Glenon, when the cheering had died down. "It has been reported to me that in the heat of battle one of our officers turned tail and fled – a sad blot on the honour of the Aquoran fleet! Naturally this matter will be fully investigated, and disciplinary action may be necessary. I'll say no more about that now, pending the outcome of the investigation."

Max glanced round and saw Lieutenant Jared, looking particularly pale and bitter, standing at the edge of the room. Jared opened his mouth as if to say something, then shut it again. He sidled through the door and quietly left the room.

"Speeches over!" Glenon said, raising his glass. "Good health to everyone!" The room soon filled with the pleasant buzz of conversation.

Max wandered over to the window. Lia followed him.

"That's quite a view," she said. "Your city is amazing. I admit it!"

"Thanks," Max said, grinning at his friend. "Hey, look at that!"

Far below, he could see the giant, mangled robotic skeleton of Drakkos being brought ashore. The Aquoran Salvage Crew had dredged it up from the bottom of the sea. Now it was being pulled on a trailer into the city. It was going to be taken apart and studied by Aquoran scientists and engineers, Max had heard.

"Looks harmless enough now," Lia said.

"They always look harmless after we've defeated them!" Max said.

A hand settled on his shoulder. Max looked up to see his dad smiling down at him.

"Well done, Max," Callum said. "I'm proud of you. So is your mother. You know that, don't you?"

"I guess so," Max said, feeling the blood rush to his cheeks. "Hey, I've got your Access card to give you." He handed it over. "Only it might not work now. I used it to deprogramme a gigantic Robobeast."

"That sounds like my son!" his father laughed. "Well, you've been busy, Max. Now it's time to relax. Have a holiday. Show Lia the sights of Aquora. No more Quests for a while, all right?"

"All right," Max said with a smile. It certainly would be nice to take things easy for a bit. The Professor was safely locked up again, and Cora Blackheart was marooned in the Lost Lagoon. All the same, he had a feeling it wouldn't be long before his next Sea Quest. He wondered what it would be...

Don't miss the next Sea Quest book,
in which Max faces

SYTHID
THE SPIDER CRAB

Read on for a sneak preview!

CHAPTER ONE

UNEXPECTED GUESTS

"Ten points!" yelled Max as his aquabowl disc struck the final floating pin and sent it bobbing across the surface of the pool.

The secluded bowling pool lay in a corner of Aquora's harbour, in the shade of the great city's silver towers and needle-sharp skyscrapers. It was surrounded by banks of seating for spectators, although they were mostly empty today. Strings of coloured lights hung everywhere, and a band was playing, adding to the festive atmosphere.

"It's a stupid game," grumbled Lia, picking up another disc, a smooth plate of white metal that flashed with blue and amber lights. So far, Lia hadn't managed to hit a single target. Using technology didn't come naturally to her – even something as simple as an aquabowl disc.

"It's fun once you've had a bit of practice," Max promised, as he pressed a button to set the targets up again.

"Fine – watch this!" declared Lia, a crafty expression coming over her face as she dived into the pool. She pulled her Amphibio mask off and let out a series of high-pitched calls.

Moments later, a shoal of blue flying fish appeared, leaping from the harbour and plunging into the pool.

Max watched as Lia used her amazing Aqua Powers to command the shoal. *That's cheating*, he thought, as one by one, the leaping fish knocked down the targets.

"*That's* how to play aquabowl!" Lia said with a grin.

"Fine, you win," Max accepted grudgingly. "But that's not really in the rules!"

It felt good to be relaxing, with the danger of their recent adventures behind them. It wasn't long since Max and Lia had defeated the Robobeast Drakkos created by his wicked uncle, the Professor. Now the Professor was safely locked up – and his associate, the terrifying pirate Cora Blackheart, was marooned in the Lost Lagoon. Life was peaceful in Aquora these days. Rivet, Max's faithful dogbot, was off somewhere in the harbour with Lia's swordfish, Spike, teaching each other their favourite underwater tricks.

Lia sprang from the pool, the Amphibio mask back over her nose and mouth, giving her the precious oxygen that all Merryn people needed to survive above water.

"Now what shall we do?" she asked. "No more silly games. Something *interesting*."

"I know what you mean," Max replied. It was great to be out of danger, but he was itching for a little bit more excitement.

As if in answer to his thoughts, his wrist communicator flashed and his mother's smiling face appeared on the screen.

"Max, someone's come to visit you," she told him. "He's waiting for you in the apartment."

"Who?" Max asked.

"You'll see." Her face vanished.

"Come on," said Lia. "I've had enough of thrashing you at aquabowl!"

COLLECT THEM ALL!

SERIES 1:

978 1 40831 848 5   978 1 40831 849 2   978 1 40831 850 8   978 1 40831 851 5

SERIES 2: THE CAVERN OF GHOSTS

978 1 40832 411 0   978 1 40832 412 7   978 1 40832 413 4   978 1 40832 414 1

SERIES 3: THE PRIDE OF BLACKHEART

978 1 40832 853 8   978 1 40832 855 2   978 1 40832 857 6   978 1 40832 859 0

SERIES 4: THE LOST LAGOON

978 1 40832 853 8   978 1 40832 855 2   978 1 40832 857 6   v

www.seaquestbooks.co.uk

LOOK OUT FOR SERIES 5:
THE CHAOS QUADRANT

SYTHID
THE SPIDER CRAB

BRUX
THE TUSKED TERROR

978 1 40833 471 3   978 1 40833 471 3

VENOR
THE SEA SCORPION

MONOTH
THE SPIKED DESTROYER

978 1 40833 475 1   978 1 40833 477 5

DON'T MISS THE NEXT SPECIAL
BUMPER EDITION: OCTOR,
MONSTER OF THE DEEP!

WIN AN EXCLUSIVE
GOODY BAG

In every Sea Quest book the Sea Quest logo is
hidden in one of the pictures. Find the logo in this book,
make a note of which page it appears on and
go online to enter the competition at

www.seaquestbooks.co.uk

Each month we will put all of the correct entries into a draw
and select one winner to receive a special Sea Quest goody bag.

You can also send your entry on a postcard to:

Sea Quest Competition, Orchard Books,
338 Euston Road, London, NW1 3BH

Don't forget to include your name and address!

GOOD LUCK

Closing Date: 28th February 2015

DARE YOU DIVE IN?

Deep in the water lurks a new breed of Beast.

If you want the latest news and exclusive Sea Quest goodies, join our Sea Quest Club!

Visit www.seaquestbooks.co.uk/club and sign up today!

IF YOU LIKE SEA QUEST, YOU'LL LOVE **BEAST QUEST!**

Series 1: COLLECT THEM ALL!

An evil wizard has enchanted the magical beasts of Avantia. Only a true hero can free the beasts and save the land. Is Tom the hero Avantia has been waiting for?

978 1 84616 483 5

978 1 84616 482 8

978 1 84616 484 2

978 1 84616 486 6

978 1 84616 485 9

978 1 84616 487 3

DON'T MISS THE
BRAND NEW SERIES OF:

Series 15: VELMAL'S REVENGE

978 1 40833 487 4

978 1 40833 489 8

978 1 40833 491 1

978 1 40833 498 5